Mr. Putter & Tabby Write the Book

CYNTHIA RYLANT

Mr. Putter & Tabby Write the Book

Illustrated by
ARTHUR HOWARD

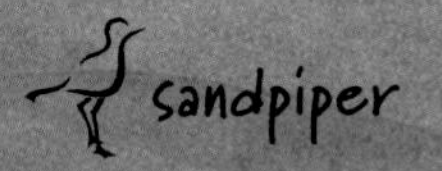

Houghton Mifflin Harcourt
Boston New York

For AJ, DJ, and EJ—C. R.

For Cyndi—A. H.

 Published in the United States by Sandpiper, an imprint of Houghton Mifflin Harcourt Publishing Company. Originally published in hardcover in the United States by Harcourt Children's Books, an imprint of Houghton MIfflin Harcourt Publishing Company, 2004.

www.hmhco.com

Library of Congress Cataloging-in-Publication Data
Rylant, Cynthia.
Mr. Putter & Tabby write the book/Cynthia Rylant; illustrated by Arthur Howard.
p. cm.
Summary: During a big snow, Mr. Putter decides to write a mystery novel,
but what he ends up with is entirely different.
[1. Authorship—Fiction. 2. Cats—Fiction.]
I. Title: Mr. Putter and Tabby write the book. II. Howard, Arthur, ill. III. Title.
PZ7.R982Mh 2004
[E]—dc22 2003019521
ISBN 978-0-15-200241-1 hc
ISBN 978-0-15-200242-8 pb

Manufactured in China

SCP 20 19 18 17 16 15
4500629978

1

An Idea

In the winter a big snow
always came to Mr. Putter's house.

Mr. Putter and his fine cat, Tabby,
liked big snows.
But they couldn't go out in them.
They were too old.
Mr. Putter might slip and break something.
Tabby might catch a bad cold.

They didn't mind staying in, though,
because Mr. Putter's house was so cozy.
It had nice soft chairs.
It had velvet pillows.
It had a fireplace.

Staying in was all right
when everything was so
soft and velvety and warm.

One day when Mr. Putter and Tabby
were inside for a big snow,
Mr. Putter got an idea.

His idea was to write a book.

He had everything a writer needed:

a soft chair,

a warm fire,

and a good cat.

And he had a pen and plenty of paper.

"I have always wanted to write a mystery novel,"

Mr. Putter said to Tabby.

So he brought out lots of paper, lit the fire,
plumped his chair,
and got ready to begin.

First he had to think of a title.

He thought

and thought

and thought.

Finally he told Tabby,
"I shall call my book
The Mystery of Lighthouse Cove."

It was a very good title.
It was full of mystery.
As a boy he had read lots of books
with titles like that.

Mr. Putter was so pleased,
he decided to fix a snack.
He went into the kitchen
and fixed a big apple salad,
a pan of corn muffins,
some custard pudding,
and a cheese ball.

Mr. Putter spent three minutes
on his title
and four hours
on his snack.

Then he took a nap.

Mystery writing was not easy work.

2

Chapter One

On the second day that he was
a mystery writer, Mr. Putter
had a nice long breakfast with Tabby
of oatmeal and tea.
Then he settled down to write again.

But first he had to stoke the fire.

Then he had to clean Tabby's ears.

Then he had to find a sweater.

Then he had to move his chair
closer to the window.
Then he had to move it back.

Then he settled down again.

He was ready to write.

Mr. Putter looked at the walls and he thought.

He thought and thought and thought.

Finally he wrote: CHAPTER ONE.

He began to think some more.
As he was thinking,
he looked out the window.
A rabbit was in the yard.
"Such a nice rabbit," Mr. Putter said to Tabby.
The rabbit made him think of Easter,
and Easter made him think of boiled eggs.

He decided to fix a snack.
He went into the kitchen and fixed
twenty boiled eggs and a vegetable stew.

Mr. Putter spent one minute on CHAPTER ONE
and three hours on eggs and stew.

Then he took a bath.

Then he took a nap.

Mystery writing wore him out.

3

Good Things

The third day that he was a mystery writer,
Mr. Putter woke up ready to write again.
He liked being a writer ready to write.

First he and Tabby had cinnamon toast and tea.

Then Mr. Putter petted Tabby
and began to think.
He looked out of his window, thinking.
He looked at his fire, thinking.
He looked at Tabby, thinking.

Mr. Putter thought how blue the sky was.
He thought how warm the fire felt.
He thought how nice it was to be with Tabby.
He thought about so many good things
that he began to write them down.

He wrote and wrote and wrote.

Mr. Putter wrote all day long.

When he finally stopped writing,
the big snow had melted.
Mr. Putter went next door with
Tabby to visit Mrs. Teaberry and
her good dog, Zeke.

They had some french-fried
butternut squash for supper.

Then Mr. Putter read *Good Things.*

When he finished,
Mrs. Teaberry said it was "enchanting."
She said Mr. Putter was
a wonderful writer.
She said she could listen forever.

“I wanted to write
The Mystery of Lighthouse Cove,”
Mr. Putter said sadly.
“But I wrote *Good Things* instead.
And I ate too much
and took too many naps.”

Mrs. Teaberry told him not to worry.
She said the world is full of mystery writers.
But writers of good things
are few and far between.

Mr. Putter did not feel so sad then.
He did not feel sad at all.
In fact, he was thrilled.
(Every writer loves a good review.)

To celebrate good reviews
and good neighbors,
Mr. Putter took Mrs. Teaberry
and Tabby and Zeke
out for vanilla malts.

And Mr. Putter had so much fun
and thought of so many good things
that he could not wait
for the next big snow...

… so he could be a writer again.

The illustrations in this book were done in pencil, watercolor,
gouache, and Sennelier pastels on 250-gram cotton rag paper.
The display type was set in Minya Nouvelle, Agenda, and Artcraft.
The text type was set in Berkeley Old Style Book.
Color separations by Colourscan Co. Pte. Ltd., Singapore
Printed by RR Donnelley, China
Production supervision by Ginger Boyer
Series cover design by Kristine Brogno and Michele Wetherbee
Cover design by Brad Barrett
Designed by Arthur Howard and Judythe Sieck